Be Patient, Abdul

To all of us who are seeking
to become more patient and to
all of you who had the patience to
assist in the development
of this book.

Author's Note

Under the hot West African sun lies a country called Sierra Leone. It has beautiful sandy beaches along its Atlantic Ocean coast. Unfortunately, most of the people who live there, including the children, don't have time to enjoy the beaches. They must work hard every day.

The history of Sierra Leone started over six centuries ago. First the Portuguese and then the British started trading and then built forts there. When slavery was stopped many Africans went home and Freetown grew. On April 27, 1961, Sierra Leone became an independent nation in the British Commonwealth.

Margaret K. McElderry Books
An imprint of Simon & Schuster Children's Publishing Division
1230 Avenue of the Americas
New York, New York 10020

Text and illustrations copyright © 1996 by Dolores Sandoval

Book design by Becky Terhune
The text of this book is set in Universe.
The illustrations were rendered in acrylic paint.
Printed and bound in the United States of America

First Edition

10 9 8 7 6 5 4 3 2 1

Library of Congress Cataloging-in-Publication Data

Sandoval, Dolores.
Be patient, Abdul / written and illustrated by Dolores Sandoval.—1st ed.
p. cm.
Summary: With the help of his younger sister, seven-year-old Abdul raises money to
go to school by selling oranges in the marketplace in Sierra Leone.
ISBN 0-689-50607-4
[1. Sierre Leone—Fiction. 2. Moneymaking projects—Fiction. 3. Brothers and sisters—Fiction.] I. Title.
PZ7.S2185Be 1994 [Fic]—dc20 93-34224
CIP AC

Be Patient, Abdul

written and illustrated by

Dolores Sandoval

Margaret K. McElderry Books

Abdul is a little boy who lives in Freetown, the capital of Sierra Leone. Abdul is seven years old and he already has a job. He sells oranges.

Abdul sells oranges because he wants to learn as much as he can.

He loves to go to school and listen to the teacher.
But in Sierra Leone schools are not free.
He sells oranges so he can help to pay his school fees.

Every day he goes out to one of the marketplaces.
He carries a big tray of oranges on his head.

Sometimes he carries it on his shoulders.
It is heavy, so he tries to sell the oranges as fast as he can.

One day Abdul felt very sad. He had to go home without selling even one orange. He tried to hold back the tears but he couldn't.

His grandmother said, "Don't cry, Abdul. You must be patient. The money will come. Tomorrow, go to King Jimmy Market. There will be a lot of people selling there too. But don't be afraid."

Next morning Abdul got up and put on the clean shirt his grandmother had ironed for him.

He was just leaving the house when his mother called him back. "Take Maryama with you, Abdul. She can help you."

Oh no! he said to himself. How can *she* help me? She's only five years old and I teach *her* everything.

But Abdul couldn't disobey his mother. All he could do was say to his sister, "Let's go, Maryama."

Maryama was quiet because she couldn't walk and talk at the same time. She had to save her breath and try to keep up with Abdul. He was walking as fast as he could, even though the heavy tray slowed him down.

When they finally got to King Jimmy Market, there were a lot of people selling all kinds of food. The food was a rainbow of colors.

There were red tomatoes, yellow peppers, green lettuce, orange yams, white rice, brown potatoes, peas and beans and lots more.

The ladies who sold them sat and gossiped. Some of them had their babies tied on their backs or sitting beside them. But all the time, they talked and laughed and called out to the people walking past to buy from them.

There were other boys and girls, too, selling groundnuts or fish they had caught, but Abdul didn't know any of them.

By the end of the day Abdul had sold only a few oranges.
"I'll never get back to school if I don't earn more money,"
he said to Maryama.

Abdul was mad.

He stuck out his jaw and kicked at pebbles as they walked
home.
No matter what Grandmother said, he *couldn't* be patient.

Maryama knew enough not to bother him about anything
right then.

That evening, Abdul's father said his prayers under the big tree in their yard. After he had finished saying them, he called the family to him.

"This Saturday," he told them, "there will be a big parade to celebrate the day that our country won its independence. Your mother will be in the parade," he said, "and we'll go and watch!"

Right away Maryama began to jump around and shout. "Will there be dancers? Will there be bands? Will there be children in the parade?"

Poppa said yes to all her questions. People would come from all over Sierra Leone.

Then he made marks in the sand so Maryama could count the number of days until Saturday.

The next day Abdul went out by himself with the oranges. He decided to walk to the big cotton tree in the center of Freetown. It was famous for its size. There were lots of people there. But not many of them wanted to buy oranges.

So Abdul earned only a few coins, and that night, when he added them to the box where he saved them, school seemed like a faraway dream.

As he left the house every day his mother would say, "Abdul, be patient. You will get back to school. The money will come." That's what his grandmother had told him too.

But each evening Abdul came home with lots of oranges and just a few coins.

How could he be patient?

One morning he had to run some errands for his mother so he was late getting started to the market.

And that day, too, he had to take Maryama with him again.

He was mad! But Momma just said, "Abdul, be patient. The money for your school will come."

When Abdul and Maryama reached the big cotton tree, Maryama was glad to sit down for a while, but Abdul walked around.

"Oranges for sale! Oranges for sale!" he called out over and over. Nothing happened.

When he came back to Maryama she was standing not far from a beautiful lady in a blue dress.

"The lady's eyes match her dress," she whispered to Abdul. Abdul told her to stop staring.

Quickly Maryama pulled up the front of her skirt to make a basket. She put as many oranges into it as she could and went over to the lady. Abdul knew she just wanted to get a closer look at the lady's blue eyes.

He was very embarrassed.

"W-w-w-would you like to buy some oranges?" Maryama
stammered.

The lady looked down at small Maryama with her skirt full
of oranges and laughed. Some of the other women and
men laughed too. Poor Abdul was even more embarrassed.

But they bought a lot of the oranges!

Abdul felt guilty. He hadn't wanted Maryama to come and now she had really helped him. Even so, the money box was not very heavy that evening. Abdul still needed to have patience.

The next day was Saturday, the day of the big parade.
Abdul wanted to see the parade but he needed to sell
oranges too.

He couldn't. Momma was ready to start out for the
stadium where the parade would begin. Poppa had left
very early to drive people in his taxi.

Maryama walked on one side of her mother. Abdul was
on the other side, and baby Alimamy was tied on his
mother's back. Grandmother stayed at home because it
was a long walk to the stadium.

When they finally got there, Momma told Abdul and
Maryama to stand by the gate and wait for their father.

Then their mother disappeared to find her place in the
parade.

At last Abdul and Maryama saw Poppa. The crowds of people were so large that Abdul had begun to wonder if his father would ever find them. "Hello, Poppa!" he said, as soon as his father arrived.

Poppa had been busy in his taxi all morning.

Poppa and Abdul and Maryama hurried in to find seats. They were lucky. They were able to squeeze in not too far from where the president was sitting.

All the dancers and musicians would perform extra specially for him, so the family would see everything well.

Some of the dancers were on stilts. They were famous and Abdul decided that he might learn to do that—if he didn't become a lawyer.

When Momma's group came by, Abdul and Maryama clapped and called to her. She stopped and waved.

They had to laugh at baby Alimamy who was bouncing along on Momma's back.

A long time later, when the parade was over, Poppa told Abdul to wait at the gate for his mother. Maryama was tired, so Poppa took her in the taxi with the passengers.

Abdul waited and he waited, but Momma didn't come. Finally he decided to ask the guard how to get to Pademba Road where he lived. It was lucky he asked because he had been sure the road was in the opposite direction.

At last Abdul got home. His grandmother had made a special supper. She cooked fufu, vegetable stew, and fish.

Momma was glad to find Abdul there when she came. She had waited at the gate and worried about him. But she decided he had gone home alone because she was so late in coming. When the parade had ended, Momma had been on the far side of the stadium and it had taken a long time to get to the gate where Abdul had been waiting.

At last Poppa arrived with Maryama. He was very happy because lots of people had wanted to ride in his taxi.

After they had eaten Grandmother's special supper, Poppa brought out the box in which Abdul kept the money he earned to pay for his school. "Count it," Poppa said.

Abdul spread the money out on the ground and counted each coin. His father had put in the taxi money he had made that day. There was enough for Abdul to go back to school!

Maryama and Abdul danced around the money box. They danced around the tree. They danced around the yard.

Abdul did not have to be patient any more.

Now he could go to school again. He would listen to the teacher. He would learn everything and he would teach it all to Maryama.

That night when Abdul ended his prayers he said, "Thank you, Allah, for the oranges to sell, for the passengers for Poppa's taxi, for my family, and, most of all, for giving me patience."